WHAT'S THE BIG IDEA?

Australian Inventions that Changed the World

Sue Lawson & Karen Tayleur

For Bruce - the most creative,
inventive problem solver I know.
And love. - S.L.

This is dedicated to my goddaughter Ella Grace
who is brimming with Big Ideas — I look forward
to seeing them come to fruition. - K.T.

First published in 2022 by

wild dog

PO Box 135
Fitzroy VIC 3065
Australia
wdog.com.au

Copyright text © Sue Lawson and Karen Tayleur 2022

Designed by Guy Holt

All rights reserved. Apart from any fair dealing for the purpose of study, research, criticism or review, as permitted under the Copyright Act, no part of this book may be reproduced by any process, stored in a retrieval system, or transmitted in any form, without permission of the copyright owner. All enquiries should be made to the publisher at the address above.

Front cover Pix by Monique, Reid Dalland, Billion Photos, art of line, Aleksandr Artt; p 1 Ridackan; p 2 Ridackan; p3 create jobs 51, UnknownLatitude Images, Goldilock Project, Meranda19; p 4 Max Topchii, Magic mine, TheFarAwayKingdom, WAYHOME studio, Daxiao Productions; p 5 Kallayanee Naloka, Oxima, ViDI Studio; p 6 Pixel-Shot, Peter Kotoff, Olha Yerofieieva; p 7 Axel Alvarez, CoolPhotoGirl, Kalah_R, alpkhan photography, skyboysv; p 8 Naeblys, Lori Malkhassian, ulegundo, FabrikaSimf; p 9 shooarts, NicoElNino, domnitsky; p 10 Life morning, Milleflore Images, Nareerat Mudngern, dinosoft; p 11 Vitezslav Valka, Reid Dalland, Tattoboo, p 12 I000s_pixels; p 13 Museums Victoria, Alesandro14, Olga_i; p 14 Africa Studio, passengerz, AlexLMX, Krishnadas, GAlexS; p 15 ViewStock, Anan Kaewkhammul, Darren Tierney; p 16 tomas del amo; p 17 Julio Macias, xshot, Youimages; p 18 Oleg Kopyov, The State Library of Victoria; p 19, State Library of New South Wales, Morphart Creation, Eric Isselee, Powerhouse Productions, Attribution 4.0 International; p 20 Museums Victoria; p 21 Guy Holt, Alena TS, Museum of Applied Arts and Sciences, Sydney; p 22 Alhovik, Creative Commons BY-NC-SA, spacezerocom, Museums Victoria; p 23 Stone36, newelle, B-D-S Piotr Marcinski, Museums Victoria; p 24 SeDmi, A9 STUDIO; p 25 Pix By Monique; p 26 Jan Schneckenhaus, Pavlo S, fotografos, Collection Mass Museum; p 27 VLADIMIR DUDKIN, Andrei Dubadzel, Loredana Crupi; p 28 Teerapun, T.Lagerwall, los_jan, EFKS; p 29 AlexLMX, CHAN Ping Chau; p 30 Collection Mass Museum, Sergey Mironov, Ljupco Smokovski; p 31 vipman, Dima Zel, Benjamin Knight; p 32 Ridackan; p 33 Ridackan; Endpaper Aleksandr Artt.

Printed and bound in China by
Everbeast Printing Investment Limited
ISBN: 9781742036267

10 9 8 7 6 5 4 3 2 1   22 23 24 25 26

Wild Dog Books acknowledges traditional owners across this great continent. We pay our respects to Elders past, present and future and thank them for their work in nurturing, sustaining and managing Country for tens of thousands of years.

FSC® MIX Paper from responsible sources FSC® C124385

FSC® is a non-profit international organisation established to promote the responsible management of the world's forests.

A catalogue record for this book is available from the National Library of Australia

WHAT'S THE BIG IDEA?
CONTENTS

- Introduction 2
- Medicine 3
- Technology 9
- Communication 11
- Transport 13
- Sport 15
- Agriculture 18
- Tools 21
- Home & Food 23
- Thanks, Great Idea 29
- Charities, Events & Services 30
- Timeline 32
- Glossary/Index 34

WHAT'S THE BIG IDEA?

INTRODUCTION

An invention is something created to solve a problem or make life easier. Inventions can start as a question: 'I wonder if there's a better way to do this?' Or they can come about by chance, which is what happened with penicillin and the stump-jump plough.

All the inventions in this book have one thing in common. They're Australian ideas. That's right, Australians have created some of the world's most amazing inventions. From ancient tools and spray-on skin to bionic ears and unique vehicles, Australians have helped change the world. Maybe it's the open space that makes Australians such a creative bunch. Or perhaps Australians have had to be inventive because they are so far from other countries.

Whatever the case, Australians have come up with some of the world's most important and life-changing inventions.

WHAT'S THE BIG IDEA?

MEDICINE

THE PACEMAKER

Dr Mark Lidwill and Dr Edgar Booth
Year: 1926
Location: Sydney

A pacemaker is a small device surgically implanted into a patient's chest. It sends electrical messages to keep the heart beating regularly.

In 1926, anaesthetist Dr Mark Lidwill and physicist Dr Edgar Booth were trying to save a baby born with heart failure. They discovered they could keep the baby's heart beating regularly by attaching electrodes to the infant and sending electrical messages to its heart. The duo's ingenuity saved the infant's life and created the world's first pacemaker.

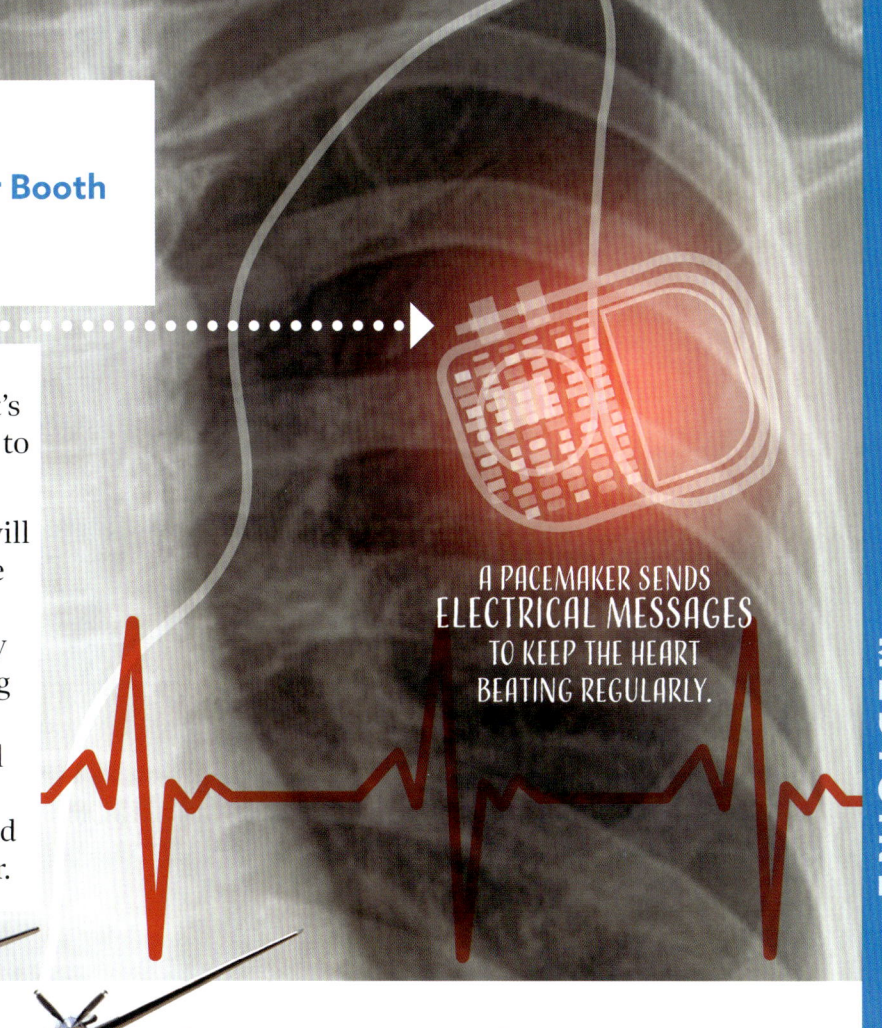

A PACEMAKER SENDS ELECTRICAL MESSAGES TO KEEP THE HEART BEATING REGULARLY.

ROYAL FLYING DOCTOR SERVICE

Reverend John Flynn
Year: 1928
Location: South Australia

While working in remote South Australia, Reverend John Flynn discovered seriously ill and injured people faced problems when trying to access medical help. He combined two new technologies – aircraft and the pedal-operated wireless radio – to create the Australian Inland Mission Aerial Medical Service. Access to the wireless radio allowed outback residents to radio for medical support. The service flew doctors and other medical staff to provide help and transport patients to hospital.

FLYNN'S CREATION, THE ROYAL FLYING DOCTOR SERVICE, STILL PROVIDES EMERGENCY CARE TO PEOPLE IN REMOTE AREAS.

3

PLASTIC EYEGLASS LENSES

Scientific Optical Laboratories
Year: 1960
Location: Adelaide

Until 1960, all eyeglasses had glass lenses. That's why we call them glasses. While glass lenses made it easier for people to see, they were heavy and, if they broke, the glass could damage eyes. Australia's Scientific Optical Laboratories created the world's first plastic lenses for eyeglasses in 1960. The plastic lenses were less scratch-resistant and 60% lighter than glass. This made them comfortable to wear and longer-lasting.

STAINLESS-STEEL BRACES

Dr Percy Raymond Begg and Arthur Wilcock
Year: 1956
Location: Adelaide/Melbourne

Teeth straightening has been a thing for thousands of years. Archaeologists even found metal wired through the teeth of Egyptian mummies.

Orthodontists once used rubber, wood, ivory and even gold to force teeth into a straighter position. The treatments hurt, usually looked bad, and were expensive.

In 1956, Adelaide orthodontist Dr Percy Raymond Begg and Victorian metallurgist Arthur Wilcock created stainless-steel wires braces. They were lighter to wear, cheaper to fit, and were more comfortable for the wearer. Begg and Wilcock's stainless-steel braces changed and improved teeth straightening worldwide.

MEDICAL USE OF PENICILLIN

Dr Howard Florey and Dr Ernst Chain
Year: 1939
Location: Australia

In 1928, Dr Alexander Fleming discovered that mould had stopped the growth of bacteria in a petri dish. Fleming investigated and found the mould produced a bacteria-killing chemical. What he first called 'mould juice' was the substance penicillin.

More than a decade later, Australian pathologist Dr Howard Florey and biochemist Dr Ernst Chain discovered penicillin could fight bacteria in the human body. Penicillin became the world's first antibiotic drug. Florey, Chain and Fleming received the Nobel Prize in Physiology or Medicine in 1945.

TODAY, ANTIBIOTICS ARE AMONG THE WORLD'S MOST PRESCRIBED MEDICATIONS.

ZINC CREAM

Faulding Pharmaceutical Company
Year: 1940
Location: Adelaide

While experimenting with sunscreen, pharmacists at Adelaide's Faulding Pharmaceutical Company discovered zinc oxide cream stopped the sun's UVA and UVB rays reaching the skin. The cream worked a little like a mirror, reflecting rays away from the skin. Also called a barrier cream, zinc cream can be used as sunscreen and to treat and prevent skin conditions such as burns, nappy rash and insect bites.

ZINC CREAM WORKED A LITTLE LIKE A MIRROR, REFLECTING RAYS AWAY FROM THE SKIN

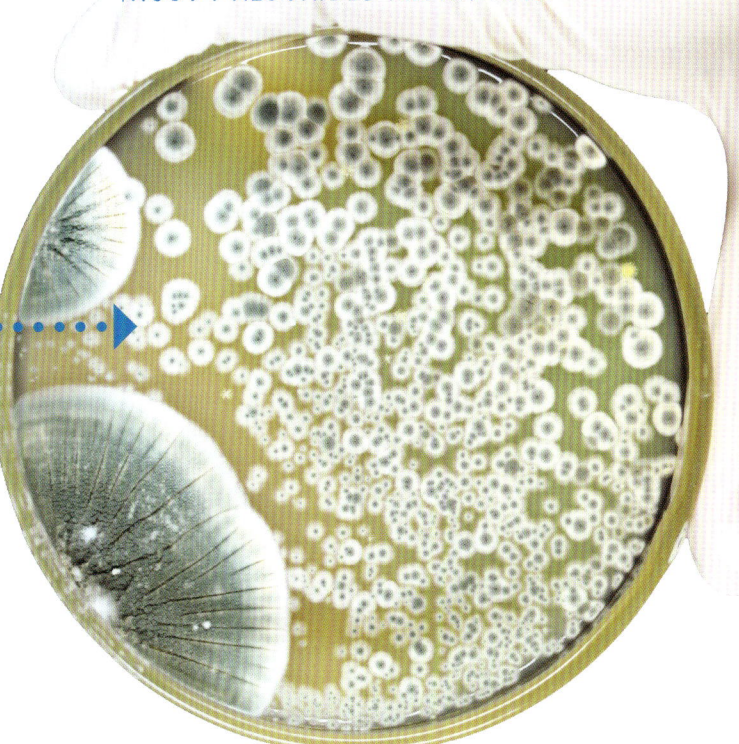

AEROGARD

Dr Doug Waterhouse
Year: 1963
Location: CSIRO

During World War II, Australian CSIRO scientist Dr Doug Waterhouse created a formula to protect Australian soldiers from malaria-carrying mosquitos and biting bugs.

The spray-on formula worked but wasn't available to the public until after Queen Elizabeth's trip to Canberra in 1963. Waterhouse sent the spray to Queen Elizabeth to make her journey more comfortable. The spray was so successful that fly-repellent manufacturer Mortein bought Waterhouse's formula and named the spray Aerogard. Aerogard has been an essential Australian item even since.

MEDICINE

SPRAY-ON SKIN

Professor Fiona Wood and Dr Marie Stoner
Year: 1993
Location: Perth

Treatment for severe burns can be a long and painful experience. Perth surgeon Professor Fiona Wood and scientist Dr Marie Stoner revolutionised burns treatment when they invented 'spray-on skin' in 1993.

Spray-on skin is a spray made from a healthy piece of skin from the burn's victim and is applied to the person's burns. The treatment is less painful and faster than other burns treatments and also reduces scarring.

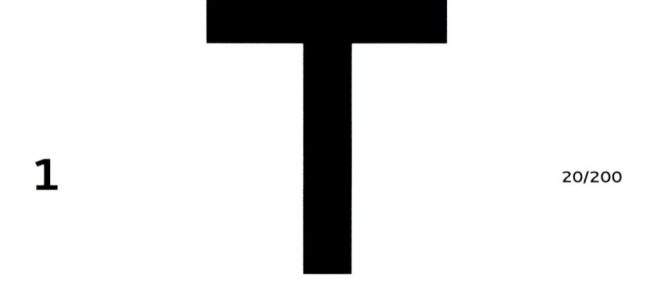

SPRAY-ON SKIN IS NOW USED AROUND THE WORLD

LONG-WEAR CONTACT LENSES

Dr Gordon Meijs and Dr Hans Griesser
Year: 1991
Location: CSIRO

AND MULTI-FOCAL CONTACT LENSES

Stephen Newman
Year: 1993
Location: Queensland

Scientists created contact lenses after experimenting with other ways to correct vision. The first contact lenses were rigid, only corrected single-zone vision problems, and had to be replaced daily, which increased the risk of eye infection and irritation. In 1991, Australian CSIRO researchers Dr Gordon Meijs and Dr Hans Griesser developed a silicone contact lens which could be worn for up to 30 days and nights without having to be changed.

Two years later, Queensland optical research scientist Stephen Newman developed multi-focal contact lenses. Today, people who need glasses have many options when it comes to improving their vision.

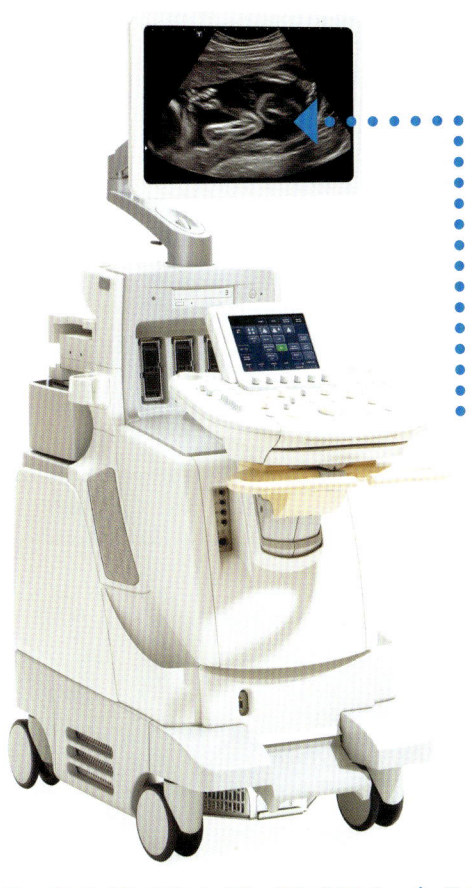

ULTRASOUND SCANNERS

Dr David Robinson and Dr George Kossoff
Year: 1961 and 1976
Location: Ausonics

Ultrasound is high-frequency sound waves that human ears can't hear. In medicine, ultrasound can create images of organs and muscles. Before the 1960s, doctors used x-rays to help diagnose patients. However, concerns about x-ray radiation led researchers to experiment with ultrasound scans. They were safer than x-rays and gave clearer pictures of soft tissue.

In 1961, Commonwealth Acoustic Laboratories colleagues Dr David Robinson and Dr George Kossoff built Australia's first ultrasound scanner. Called the CAL Echoscope, the scanner created clear images and was safe for pregnant women and their babies.

In 1976, Australian researchers at Ausonics invented an ultrasound scanner that showed images on a screen. This changed the way medical staff cared for pregnant women and their babies and improved diagnosis in many medical areas.

COCHLEAR IMPLANT

Professor Graeme Clark
Year: 1978
Location: Melbourne

Melbourne University professor, Graeme Clark, was inspired to invent the cochlear implant – or bionic ear – after watching the loneliness and frustration of his deaf father.

Clark, an ear, nose and throat surgeon, started work on the cochlear in 1967. He created a device that turned speech into electrical messages and sent those messages to nerves in the inner ear. The device allowed severely and profoundly deaf people to hear and helped them to speak. Clark implanted the first device into a patient in 1978.

TODAY, MORE THAN
20,000 PEOPLE
HAVE COCHLEAR IMPLANTS

MEDICINE

RELENZA INFLUENZA TREATMENT

Monash University and the CSIRO
Year: 1996
Loctaion: Melbourne

Influenza, or the common flu, affects up to 500 million people each year. It is particularly dangerous to elderly people and those with chronic health problems.

In 1996, Melbourne's Monash University and CSIRO scientists developed Relenza, the world's first drug to tackle the flu. Relenza reduces flu symptoms, including stuffy nose, sore throat, fever and aches. It also helps patients recover faster. The inhaled medication traps the virus and stops it from spreading.

THE COMMON FLU AFFECTS UP TO **500 MILLION PEOPLE** EACH YEAR

CERVICAL CANCER VACCINES

Professor Ian Frazer and Dr Jian Zhou
Year: 2006
Loctaion: Brisbane

In the 1980s, German researchers discovered the link between the Human Papillomavirus (HPV) and cancer. HPV is a virus caught by men and women and can cause cervical cancer in women.

Australia's Professor Ian Frazer and Chinese virologist Dr Jian Zhou spent 15 years creating Gardasil, a vaccine to prevent HPV. The vaccine protects men and women from 70% of HPV infections. Patients received the first HPV vaccine in 2006. Today, more than 80 countries have HPV vaccine programs.

WHAT'S THE BIG IDEA?
TECHNOLOGY

WIRELESS LOCAL AREA NETWORK (WLAN)

CSIRO Team – Dr John O'Sullivan, Dr Terry Percival, Diet Ostry, Dr Graham Daniels and Dr John Deane

Year: 1992
Location: CSIRO

WLAN is a wireless connection that connects devices such as computers, smartphones or tablets to the internet and other devices. Research teams across the world created wireless internet capabilities, but Australian inventors are responsible for the wireless internet we enjoy today.

During the 1990s, scientists from CSIRO worked with the problem of 'reverberation' — where radio waves bounced off objects in the environment, distorting the signal. After pioneering research in radioastronomy, the team solved the reverberation issue and the first commercial wi-fi products became available around the year 2000.

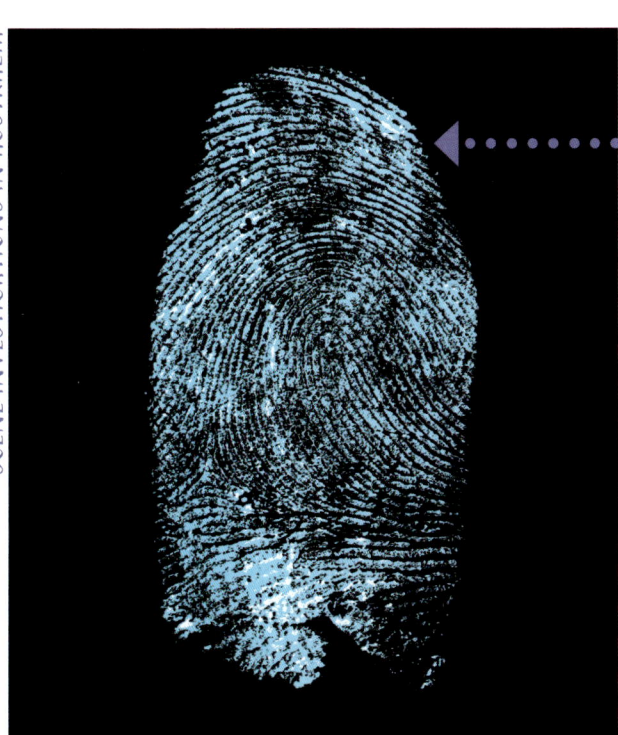

POLILIGHT FORENSIC LAMP

Dr Pierre Margot, Prof Ron Warrener, Prof Hilton Kobus, Milutin Stoilovic and Prof Chris Lennard

Year: 1989
Location: Canberra

Forensic investigators can use a Polilight lamp to detect evidence such as fingerprints, bodily fluid or even document forgeries.

The search for an alternative technology to traditional fingerprint detection began at the Australian National University in early 1980. The concept, originally known as a Unilight, sold to Rofin Australia Pty Ltd. Rofin went on to develop it into the Polilight we know today. The Polilight, or a variation of it, is used in 98 per cent of crime scene investigations in Australia and by law enforcement agencies around the world.

THE POLILIGHT IS USED IN 98 PER CENT OF CRIME SCENE INVESTIGATIONS IN AUSTRALIA

POLYMER BANK NOTES

Reserve Bank, CSIRO and Professor David Solomon

Year: 1980

Location: CSIRO

When colour photocopiers were introduced in 1967, there was a direct increase in forgeries of the Australian $10 note. To counter the forgeries, the Reserve Bank collaborated with David Solomon's CSIRO team to create polymer money that was harder to replicate and lasted 10 times longer than paper notes. The first polymer note was the $10 note, which was issued during 1988. In 1996, Australia became the first country to have a full series of polymer banknotes. Worn out polymer banknotes are recycled and made into plastic compost bins and plumbing parts.

TODAY, GOOGLE MAPS IS THE MOST WIDELY USED MAPPING PLATFORM IN THE WORLD.

GOOGLE MAPS

Where 2 Technologies

Lars Rasmussen, Jens Rasmussen Stephen Ma, Noel Gordon

Year: 2005

Location: Sydney

Australians Stephen Ma and Noel Gordon and Danish brothers Lars and Jens Rasmussen teamed up in Sydney in 2003 to establish a mapping company called Where 2 Technologies. Where 2 Technologies approached Google with an idea for a mapping system. Google bought the company in 2004. A year later Google launched Google Maps. This web-based mapping and navigation platform provides turn-by-turn directions, real-time traffic updates, satellite views and more.

TECHNOLOGY

WHAT'S THE BIG IDEA?

COMMUNICATION & STORYTELLING

YIDAKI

Yolngu people
Location: North-East Arnhem Land

Yidakis are a type of drone pipe, more commonly known by their generic name, didgeridoo or didgeridu. The yidaki is connected to the law and ceremony of the Yolngu people of North-East Arnhem Land. Yidakis are created from stringybark trees hollowed out by termites. Bark layers are stripped from the trunk of the tree, the hollow is cleaned out and a beeswax mouthpiece is added to the smaller end. The yidaki requires a circular breathing technique. Considered a sacred instrument, it is used for songs that are passed down from generation to generation. According to cultural law, only men can play the yidaki.

FIRST FULL-LENGTH FEATURE FILM

The Story of the Kelly Gang
Financed by John Tait, Nevin Tait, Charles Tait, Millard Johnson and William Gibson.
Directed by Charles Tait
Year: 1906
Location: Melbourne

On Boxing Day 1906, the first multi-reel, full-length feature film, *The Story of the Kelly Gang*, opened at the Athenaeum Theatre in Melbourne. The film took six months and £1000 to make. Released 26 years after Ned Kelly was hanged, the film was controversial because it painted the police as the 'villains', and Kelly as a 'poor victim of circumstance'. At each screening, actors behind the screen added their voices to the film while boys backstage created sound effects. The film toured Australia and even screened in New Zealand and England.

COMMUNICATION & STORYTELLING

TELEPHANE

Henry Sutton
Year: 1880
Location: Ballarat

Ballarat-born Henry Sutton was full of good ideas. Home-schooled by his mother until he was 11, Sutton had no formal education but taught himself scientific theories. A paper he wrote at the age of 14 on the theory of heavier-than-air flight was published several years later in the *Royal Aeronautical Journal of Britain*. Sutton invented the first rechargeable battery in his early 20s, and his invention, 'the telephane,' transmitted a faint image from the Melbourne Cup along telegraph wires in 1885. Sutton abandoned the telephane after becoming convinced that moving images could be transmitted wirelessly, as they are today. John Logie Baird used Henry's telephane principles to create and patent the first 'television'.

TRAEGAR PEDAL WIRELESS

Alfred Traegar
Year: 1928
Location: Queensland

Alfred Traegar was only 12 when he built a telephone line at his home. Traegar's interest in communication continued into adulthood and he built crystal sets, valve radios and transceivers and earned his radio operator's Amateur Operators Proficiency Certificate. In 1926, Reverend John Flynn, the founder of the Royal Flying Doctor Service, recruited Traegar to develop a simple radio that was easy to power and operate. Traegar invented the pedal-powered radio, which offered affordable and effective communication between the Royal Flying Doctor Service and people in remote areas of Australia. A person pumping bicycle pedals powered the radio, leaving the operator's hands free to send Morse code. The addition of a typewriter keyboard in 1931 made the radio easier to use. Traegar's wireless also helped establish the School of the Air in 1951, providing schooling for children in the outback and remote areas of Australia.

WHAT'S THE BIG IDEA?
TRANSPORT

CRANKLESS ENGINE

Anthony Michell
Year: 1920
Location: Melbourne

Engineer Anthony George Maldon Michell invented an alternative to the combustion engine. Called the crankless engine, it had fewer moving parts than combustion engines, was lighter and 10 per cent more fuel efficient. Michell travelled to America to convince car makers to replace combustion engines with his engine. However, the cost of changing outweighed the benefits.

While it didn't overtake combustions engines, the crankless engine was popular for gas engines.

INFLATABLE ESCAPE SLIDE

Jack Grant
Year: 1965
Location: Sydney

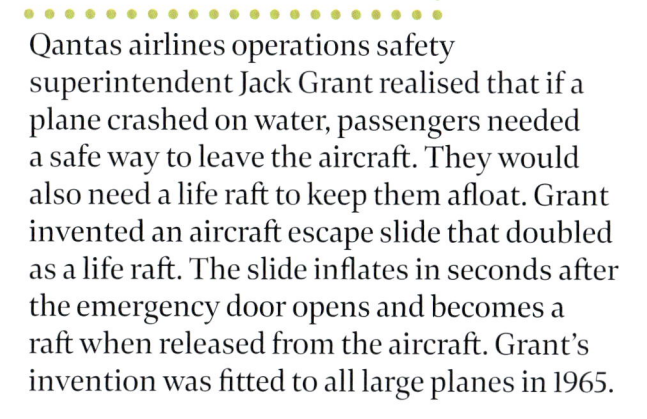

Qantas airlines operations safety superintendent Jack Grant realised that if a plane crashed on water, passengers needed a safe way to leave the aircraft. They would also need a life raft to keep them afloat. Grant invented an aircraft escape slide that doubled as a life raft. The slide inflates in seconds after the emergency door opens and becomes a raft when released from the aircraft. Grant's invention was fitted to all large planes in 1965.

THE UTE

Lewis Brandt
Year: 1934
Location: Geelong

In 1933, a Gippsland farmer's wife wrote to the Ford Motor Company in Geelong. Her family needed a car to take the family to church on Sundays and a truck to carry the pigs to market on Mondays. However, the family couldn't afford a truck and a car. Could Ford help?

Lewis Brandt, a 23-year-old designer, had the answer. Brandt modified the 1933 Ford Coupe and added a 1.6-metre tray that could carry 550 kilograms. Brandt's vehicle became the first utility vehicle, or ute, the forerunner to today's pick-up trucks.

Brandt's Ford Coupe Utility, nicknamed The Kangaroo Chaser, went on sale in 1934. Ford stopped manufacturing utes in Australia in 2017.

SAFE-N-SOUND BABY CAPSULE

Bob Botell and Bob Heath

Year: 1984

Location: Adelaide

In 1984, Australians Bob Botell and Bob Heath invented the Safe-n-Sound Baby Capsule to keep babies safe in car crashes. The capsule has two parts, an outer shell and a bassinet. The shell, which is fitted to a car's backseat, spreads the force of impact to protect the baby if the car stops suddenly or crashes. The bassinet, which cradles the baby, keeps it safe and can be used as a baby carrier.

BLACK BOX FLIGHT RECORDER

Dr David Warren

Year: 1953

Location: Melbourne

David Warren was only 9 years old when his father died in an aircraft accident in 1934. The cause of the crash was a mystery. In 1953, Dr Warren – now a chemist – investigated the crash of the world's first jetliner, a de Havilland DH 106 Comet. This investigation led him to invent the Black Box Flight Recorder.

The Black Box Flight Recorder records flight data, including the plane's direction, cabin temperature and fuel gauges. It also tapes cockpit and engine noise and conversations. Built from material that survives explosions, fire and salt water, the device is usually located near the plane's tail. The recorders are orange, not black, to make them easier to find in debris.

TODAY ALL COMMERCIAL PLANES MUST HAVE A BLACK BOX RECORDER.

PASSPORT SECURITY

Graeme Mann

Year: 1995

Location: 3M Innovative Properties Company

Today's passports have the latest security technology, thanks to Australian Graeme Mann.

Mann worked with polymer banknote technology to create a clear, tamper-proof laminate sticker, which is on every Australian passport. The laminate contains the passport holder's photograph, personal information and passport number. If peeled off, the information is lost. Mann's invention includes holographic images, which are difficult to copy, and features that only show up under ultra-violet light.

TRANSPORT

BABY ON BOARD

WHAT'S THE BIG IDEA?
SPORT

CROUCH START FOR SPRINT RACES

Bobby McDonald
Year: 1887
Location: Sydney

Also known as the 'kangaroo start', or 'sitting style' race start.

There is dispute about who invented this style of race start position. A popular theory in Australia is that Yorta Yorta runner Bobby McDonald was the first to use the crouch start. He used the position one race day in 1887 to counter strong winds that left him feeling chilled. From that day, McDonald continued to use the stance and it was eventually taken up by other runners. The style is now used by runners across the world, although many argue it provides little to no advantage over the standing start.

THE ICONIC LIFESAVING REEL WAS PHASED OUT OF SERVICE IN 1994.

SURF LIFESAVING REEL

Percy Flynn, Sig Fullwood, Lyster Ormsby, 1906 Olding & Parker, coachbuilders, redesign, 1907
Year: 1906
Loctaion: Sydney

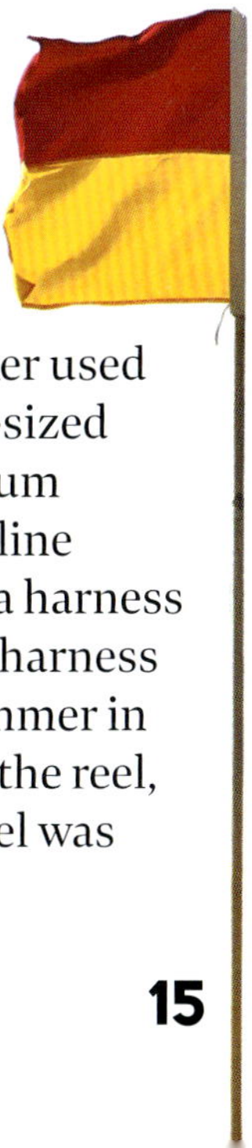

A model made from a cotton reel and hairpins was the inspiration for the lifesaving reel. Bondi Surf Bathers Life Saving Club foundation members Percy Flynn, Sig Fullwood and Lyster Ormsby built the model in 1906. Coachbuilders Olding & Parker used the model as reference to build a full-sized surf reel. The first reel was a cedar drum mounted on a wooden frame. A rope line wound around the drum attached to a harness made with cork. A lifesaver wore the harness when swimming out to rescue a swimmer in danger. It took five people to operate the reel, line and belt. The iconic lifesaving reel was phased out of service in 1994.

TODAY, SPEEDO SWIMWEAR IS MADE OF NYLON/ELASTANE.

SURF SKI

Harry McLaren
Year: 1912
Location: Port Macquarie

Fifteen-year-old Harry McLaren loved the water and working with wood. After ocean waves dumped him off his duck canoe in 1912, McLaren designed a kayak that was tapered at the back and had a spring at the front. This made it easier for the craft to shoot through waves. McLaren drew up plans for the kayak but was unable to afford the patent fees. Harry Crackanthorp, who used one of McLaren's surf skis, went on to claim credit for the invention. The surf ski revolutionised surf lifesaving and was responsible for the popularity of ocean racing.

RACER BACK COSTUME - SPEEDO

Alexander MacRae
Year: 1928
Location: Sydney

MacRae Hosiery became a business success supplying the Australian Imperial Force with socks during World War I. In 1928, the company manufactured a one-piece cotton bathing suit. Called a racer back costume, the new bathing suit might have been the first non-woollen bathing outfit invented. The suit allowed swimmers greater movement around their arms. An employee — Captain Parsonson — created the Speedo brand name, suggesting the slogan 'Speed on in your Speedos'.

SPORT

STUMP-CAM

Geoff Healy and John Porter
Year: 1980
Location: TCN Channel 9

After the success of the TCN Channel 9 Stump Mic, introduced in the late 1970s, Stump-cam followed in the early 1980s. The forward-stump facing camera, housed in the middle stump, gave a batter's view of an approaching bowled ball and the subsequent shot played. The stumps have had a recent addition with the inclusion of the back-facing camera on the same middle stump. A radio transmitter is in a ground cavity behind the stumps. Once a photo is taken, this transmitter sends the images to a control room via radio waves. Today, Stump-cams, along with Stump Mics, have become an invaluable tool to help judge player dismissals.

ZING BAILS — FLASHING CRICKET STUMPS AND BAILS

Bronte Eckermann
Year: 2012
Location: Zing International

The Australian cricket T20 Big Bash League was responsible for bright uniforms and flashy play when it launched in 2011. A year later, things got even flashier with the introduction of flashing LED stumps and bails. The stumps and bails have small LED circuits that light up to register contact. The bails also light up within 1000th of a second when dislodged from their stump groove. Industrial designer Bronte Eckermann created the flashing wickets after watching his daughter play with a ball that lit up when she threw it.

RACE-CAM

Geoff Healy and John Porter
Year: 1979
Location: ATN Channel 7

The Australian Seven Network developed the technology for Race-cam, a live broadcasting video camera system used mainly in motor racing. The son of engineer Geoff Healey inspired the invention when he placed a camera on the car dashboard during a trip to school. Race-cam allows a televised driver-view of the race and commentary from the driver. Since its creation, Race-Cam has developed to include Bumpercam, Roofcam, and Footcam. The technology has also expanded to other sports, including basketball and snow skiing.

SINCE ITS CREATION, RACE-CAM HAS DEVELOPED TO INCLUDE BUMPERCAM, ROOFCAM, AND FOOTCAM.

SPORT

WHAT'S THE BIG IDEA?
AGRICULTURE

FISH AND EEL TRAPS
Australia's First Nations People

Australia's First Nations People, members of the world's longest continuing civilisation, invented fish and eel traps. These are the oldest form of aquaculture. Traps in Victoria are carbon dated at 6600 years old, making them older than the Egyptian pyramids.

To create the traps, First Nations People built sophisticated channels and dams with rocks and branches. They trapped fish and eels in woven nets and directed others to ponds where they were held until needed for food. First Nations People also smoked eels and fish to preserve them to trade with other clans. They freed young or breeding fish to ensure a continuous supply in the future.

FIRE STICK FARMING
Australia's First Nations People

Australia's First Nations People used fire to manage Country for more than 60,000 years. They used fire to clear land, which made soil more fertile, helped germinate seeds and encouraged new growth. This type of farming, called fire stick farming, reduced leaf litter and undergrowth and prevented bushfires.

Traditional owners' deep understanding of Country ensured they chose the right time and place to burn.

AUSTRALIA'S FIRST NATIONS PEOPLE USED FIRE TO MANAGE COUNTRY FOR MORE THAN 60,000 YEARS.

MECHANICAL SHEARS

Fred Wolseley
Year: 1877
Loctaion: Walgett Euroka Station

Until 1877, shearers used hand-operated shears to cut wool from sheep. The tools made shearing slow, back-breaking work. In the 1860s, woolgrower Fred Wolseley experimented with other ways to shear sheep. In 1877, at his Walgett Euroka Station, Wolseley installed mechanised handpieces. These cut with a lateral, or sideways, movement and allowed shearers to cut faster and reduced stress on their backs. Wolseley's invention, powered by horses attached to a belt and pulley and later by engines, changed the wool industry.

CIRCULAR MOVEMENT MECHANICAL SHEARS

David Unaipon
Year: 1909
Location: Ngarrindjeri nation

In 1909, Ngarrindjeri inventor, preacher and author, David Unaipon added his own invention to the handpieces. Unaipon's addition allowed shearing machinery to cut in a circular movement, which enabled shearers to cut three-times closer to the sheep's skin. This meant heavier fleeces and more money for graziers. Closer shearing also meant graziers could shear flocks once a year, instead of three times. Modern mechanical shears still use Unaipon's design.

AGRICULTURE

STUMP-JUMP PLOUGH

Richard and Clarence Smith
Year: 1876
Location: South Australia

The first Europeans used English tools to clear trees, plant crops and build fences in Australia. Their equipment could not cope with the tough conditions and breakdowns were common.

When South Australian brothers Richard and Clarence Smith's plough hit a stump and broke a bolt, they discovered they could still use the plough and that instead of becoming stuck or breaking, it jumped obstacles, such as tree stumps.

The brothers experimented and developed the stump-jump plough, which Richard named 'The Vixen'.

MECHANICAL GRAIN STRIPPER

John Ridley
Year: 1843
Location: South Australia

A bumper wheat crop inspired South Australian flour mill owner John Ridley to invent the world's first mechanical grain stripper. Ridley knew that sickles and scythes were not the most efficient tools to harvest grain. He began work on a machine to strip wheat from stalks and keep the grain dry. In 1843 he created a harvesting machine that saved farmers time and gathered more grain to sell. The horse-drawn harvester's nicknames included 'The Ridley Reaper' and 'The Stripper'.

WHAT'S THE BIG IDEA?
TOOLS

STAYSHARP KNIFE AND SCABBARD MK1
Dennis Jackson and Stuart Devlin
Year: 1969
Location: Melbourne

When a US market survey in 1964 showed that 80% of Americans did not know how to sharpen a knife, Australian Dennis Jackson had an idea: What if he created a knife that sharpened itself? Jackson got to work inventing a spring-loaded sharpening block housed in a scabbard. Every time the knife was pulled out or pushed into the scabbard, the knife was sharpened.

When Stuart Devlin, the designer of the Australian decimal coins, was brought into the project, he created the knife's handle and plastic sheath, or scabbard. The 'Staysharp' knife was mass produced and launched Australia-wide in 1970.

SHEPHERD'S CASTORS
George Shepherd
Year: 1946
Location: Melbourne

George Shepherd, a wealthy Melbourne oil company executive, would often sit in a big club sofa chair when playing cards. The tiny castor wheels attached to the bottom of the chair were too small to easily move it around. This annoyed George so much that he spent five years perfecting a castor wheel with an angled axis, bearing, oil trap and enclosed case to keep the mechanism dust-free. Shepherd handmade 60 different versions before he was happy with the final design. More than 300 million Shepherd's Castors have sold across the world. Some of Shepherd's fortune paid for the Shepherd Foundation – a medical diagnostic centre.

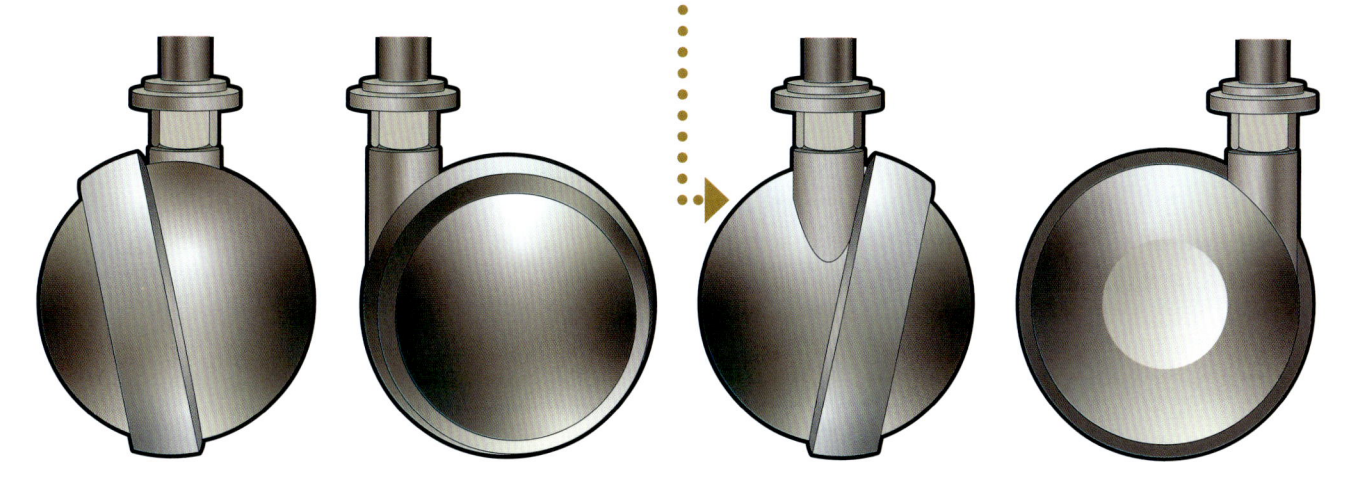

MORE THAN 300 MILLION SHEPHERD'S CASTORS HAVE SOLD ACROSS THE WORLD.

THE NOTEPAD

J A Birchall
Year: 1902
Location: Launceston

In 1844, the A W Birchall & Sons store opened in Launceston, selling books, stationery and fancy goods. At the time, four sheets of parchment or paper were folded to create eight leaves and sold in a folded stack of 24 pages called a quire. In 1902, J A Birchall thought there should be a more convenient way to sell and use writing paper. Birchall's solution was to cut the sheets in half, back the stack of paper sheets with cardboard and glue them at the top to keep them together. Birchall called his invention the Silver City Writing Tablet, a fancy name for a notepad.

WOOMERA/MIRU

Australia's First Nations People

The woomera, or miru, is a spear-throwing device usually made from mulga wood, spinifex resin and, sometimes, quartz rock. The tool helps launch a spear at a greater speed and force than by arm and hand alone. The shape and style of the woomera, or miru varies across First Nations People. The device is often shaped like narrow long bowls, which allows it to be used for other purposes, such as gathering small food items. The end of the device is covered with spinifex resin. Some users insert a sharp piece of quartz rock into the resin for cutting and sharpening other tools.

ELECTRIC DRILL

Arthur Arnot and William Brain
Year: 1889
Location: Melbourne

Arthur Arnot and William Brain created the original electric drill for drilling rock faces and coal shafts in Australia's mining industry. The drill helped speed up the mining process and required fewer workers for the same result. The drill required two hands for operation, was made of steel, and powered by an electric cable. The drill was so heavy it needed to be rested on a stable surface while the users directed the drill bit. Water cooled the drill bit to stop it from overheating.

WHAT'S THE BIG IDEA?

HOME & FOOD

MECHANICAL ICE MAKER

James Harrison
Year: 1854
Location: Melbourne

Ice hasn't always come from the refrigerator. In the 1800s, ice cut from ponds and streams in the United States and Norway was stored in ice houses before being shipped around the world, including to Australia. James Harrison designed and built the first mechanical ice-making machine in 1854. Harrison, an editor at the time, stumbled upon the idea when he used sulphuric ether to clean movable type. He noticed that the metal type felt cold when the ether fluid evaporated. Harrison took out a patent on his vapour-compression refrigeration system and called it a refrigerating machine. Harrison established the Victoria Ice Works in 1859. At the Melbourne Exhibition in 1873, he proved that months-old frozen meat was still edible once thawed. His refrigeration system is still an essential key to today's refrigerators.

COOLGARDIE SAFE

Arthur McCormick
Year: 1890
Location: Coolgardie

Arthur McCormick created this early 'refrigerator' in 1890 at Coolgardie in Western Australia. The source for his idea was a bushman's hessian bag hanging from a tree. Some believe explorer Thomas Mitchell adopted this method after observing the way First Nations People used kangaroo skins to carry water.

The Coolgardie used evaporative cooling to extend the life of food, while protecting it from insects and scavengers. This original refrigerator consisted of a cabinet, usually made of metal or timber. A tank at the top of the cabinet was filled with water, and fabric strips hung down from the tank to wet the hessian-covered sides of the cabinet. The 'cooling magic' occurred when breezes evaporated water from the hessian sides of the safe, absorbing the heat from the air around it.

HOME & FOOD

23

GRANNY SMITH APPLE

Maria Smith
Year: 1868
Location: Ryde, NSW

Legend has it that an apple seedling grew on Maria Smith's farm at Ryde, New South Wales, after she threw French crab-apple cores out her kitchen window. Another story has Maria, known locally as 'Granny', throwing out the cores and other kitchen compost near her garden creek. What is undisputed is that Smith created a new apple, which was good for cooking and eating straight from the tree. After Maria and her husband Thomas died, Edward Gallard bought the Smith farm and cultivated more 'Granny Smith' apple trees. Today Granny Smith apples are grown in Australia, New Zealand, the United States and Europe.

MORE THAN ONE MILLION PINK LADY TREES WERE PLANTED IN AUSTRALIA BY 1996.

CRIPPS PINK APPLE (PINK LADY)

John Cripps
Year: 1973
Location: Western Australia

John Cripps worked at the Western Australia Department of Agriculture with grapevine rootstock, but his side interest was apple breeding. Cripps decided to cross Golden Delicious and Lady Williams apples to create a new variety of apple, known as the Cripps Pink, or Pink Lady. More than one million Pink Lady trees were planted in Australia by 1996, and they are now grown in more than 15 countries, with apple sales to more than 30 countries worldwide.

HOME & FOOD

THE HILLS HOIST ROTARY CLOTHESLINE

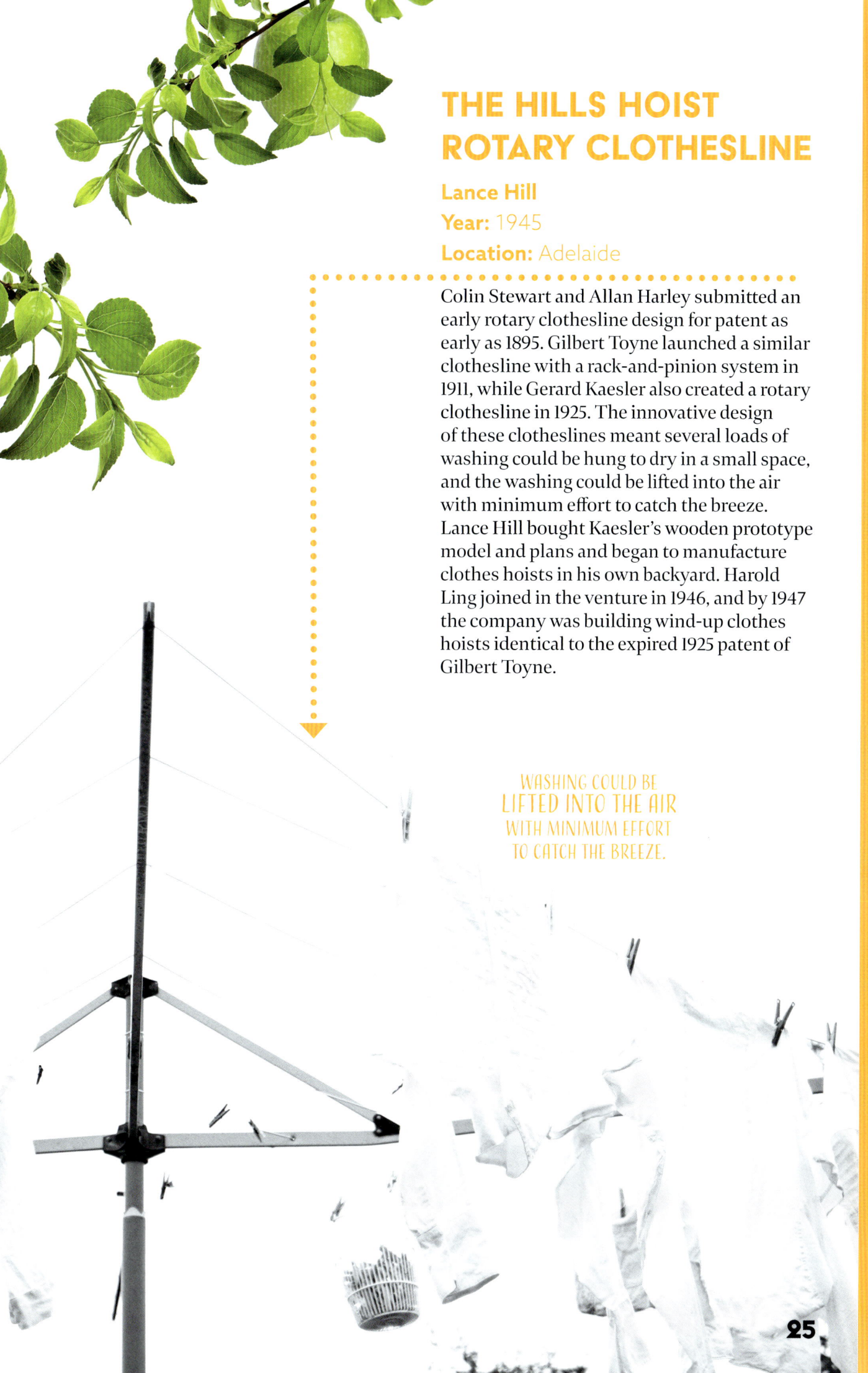

Lance Hill
Year: 1945
Location: Adelaide

Colin Stewart and Allan Harley submitted an early rotary clothesline design for patent as early as 1895. Gilbert Toyne launched a similar clothesline with a rack-and-pinion system in 1911, while Gerard Kaesler also created a rotary clothesline in 1925. The innovative design of these clotheslines meant several loads of washing could be hung to dry in a small space, and the washing could be lifted into the air with minimum effort to catch the breeze. Lance Hill bought Kaesler's wooden prototype model and plans and began to manufacture clothes hoists in his own backyard. Harold Ling joined in the venture in 1946, and by 1947 the company was building wind-up clothes hoists identical to the expired 1925 patent of Gilbert Toyne.

WASHING COULD BE LIFTED INTO THE AIR WITH MINIMUM EFFORT TO CATCH THE BREEZE.

HOME & FOOD

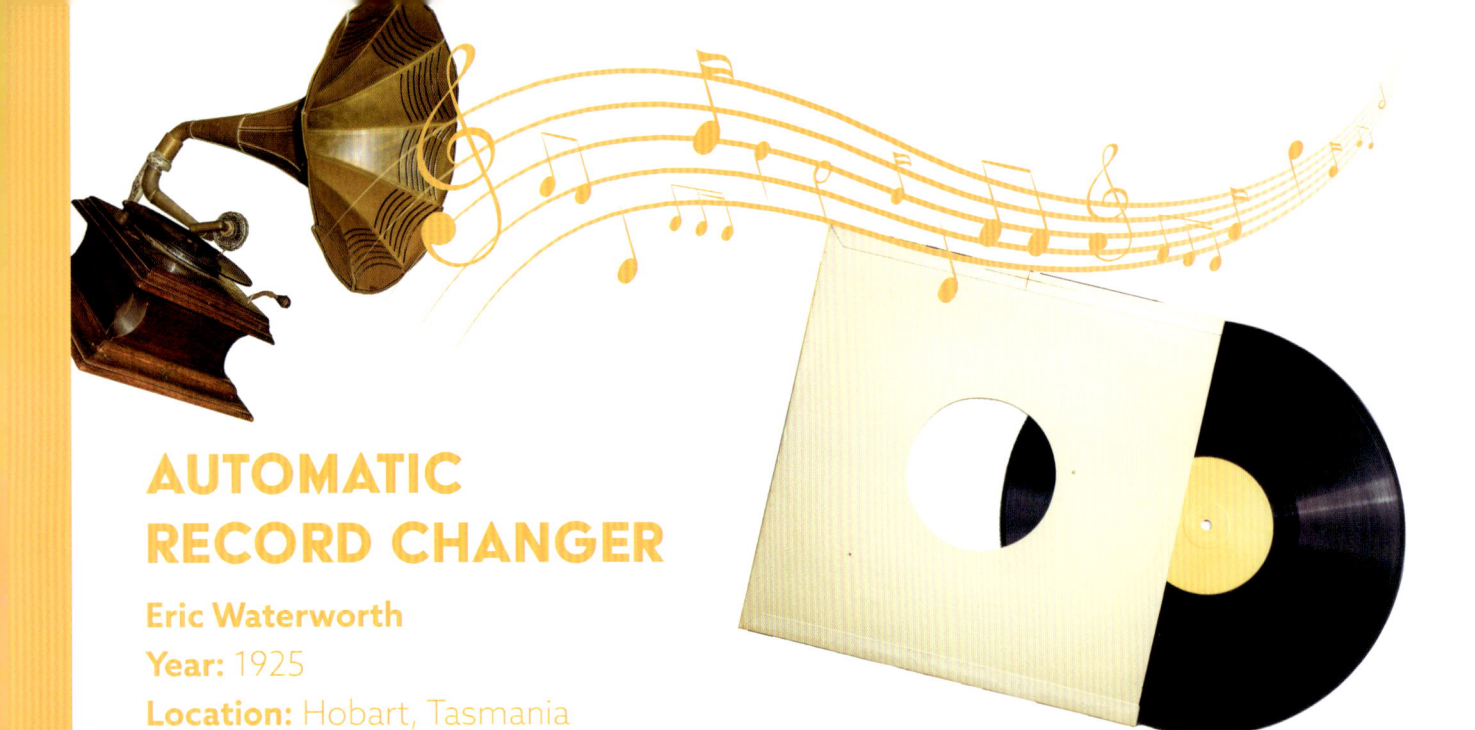

AUTOMATIC RECORD CHANGER

Eric Waterworth
Year: 1925
Location: Hobart, Tasmania

While the invention of the 'phonograph' brought music to sitting rooms in the early 1920s, it was annoying to have to 'turn' the record to hear the other side or to 'change' the record for another one. At the age of 20, Eric Waterworth patented an automatic record-changer. The design allowed for up to six vinyl records to be played in sequence before needing any intervention from the listener. In 1928, Waterworth sold the patent for the steeped centre spindle design to the Symphony Gramophone and Radio Co Ltd in London.

SPLAYD

William McArthur
Year: 1943
Location: Sydney

The Splayd is described as an 'all-in-one combination knife, fork and spoon gracefully fashioned'. It has a straight cutting edge on both sides of the fork tines, and a cupped centre. The idea for the Splayd came about during a garden party when William McArthur noticed people struggling with standard cutlery while trying to eat from the plates in their laps. In 1960, the design was sold to Stokes Pty Ltd, an Australian tableware manufacturer. The design was not mass marketed until 1962, around the time when it became popular to eat in front of the television. More than five million Splayds have sold since they were first created.

MORE THAN FIVE MILLION SPLAYDS HAVE SOLD SINCE THEY WERE FIRST CREATED.

VEGEMITE

Dr Cyril P Callister
Year: 1922
Location: Melbourne

Marmite is a spreadable paste made from a yeast extract and was popular in Australia in the early 1900s. In 1919, the Fred Walker Company hired chemist Dr Cyril P Callister to create Australia's own tasty, spreadable paste made from brewer's yeast. The company launched a national competition to name the spread, and 'Vegemite' was the winner. In 1935, Vegemite was as a staple ration for the Australian Infantry Forces during World War II and was rationed Australian-wide during this time. By the late 1940s, nine out of 10 Australian homes had a jar of Vegemite in their pantry. The one billionth jar of Vegemite was produced in 2008.

VEGEMITE FOR BEGINNERS

VEGEMITE FOR REGULAR CONSUMERS

VEGEMITE FOR THOSE TAKING A DARE

THE ONE BILLIONTH JAR OF VEGEMITE WAS PRODUCED IN 2008.

HOME & FOOD

27

DUAL-FLUSH TOILET

Bruce Thompson
Year: 1980
Location: Adelaide

DUAL-FLUSH TOILETS CAN SAVE UP TO 11,000 LITRES OF WATER PER PERSON PER YEAR.

Australia is the driest continent in the world, which is why Australians are keen to save water wherever possible, including in the toilet! Years ago, people would place a brick in the toilet cistern to reduce the amount of water to fill and flush the toilet. This often ended up damaging the toilet. In 1980, Bruce Thompson, of Adelaide business Caroma, developed the Duoset cistern with two buttons, one for a full flush and the other for a half flush. Thompson's 1980 version was the first practical implementation of the dual-flush toilet. It has been estimated that dual-flush toilets can save up to 11,000 litres of water per person per year.

VICTA LAWNMOWER

Mervyn Richardson
Year: 1952
Location: Milperra

The idea for the Victa lawnmower came to Mervyn Richardson after he watched a demonstration of the 'Mowall' rotary-blade lawnmower, which required two people to operate. In August 1952, Richardson hit upon the idea of adding an engine to drive the rotating blades. His prototype, made from a jam tin, billycart wheels and scrap metal, could cut fine grass, as well tougher and longer grass and weeds. By 1958, Richardson's company, Victa Mowers Pty Ltd, was building more than 140,000 mowers a year. The Victa lawnmower is such an Australian icon that it featured in the Olympic Games in 2000.

HOME & FOOD

WHAT'S THE BIG IDEA?
THANKS, GREAT IDEA

PRE-PAID POSTAGE

James Raymond
Year: 1838
Location: New South Wales

In the early 1800s, the person who received a letter paid for its postage, not the person who sent it. And if you didn't have the money to pay for the letter, you didn't get it. In 1837, Roland Hill proposed a complete change to the postal system in the UK, but his ideas were rejected. However, in the colony of New South Wales, postmaster James Raymond took up one of Hill's ideas. James introduced the first pre-paid postage in the form of envelopes embossed with the seal of the colony. England introduced the pre-paid self-adhesive stamp in 1840 and the colonies officially adopted stamps in 1848, after the pre-paid NSW envelopes proved unpopular with the public.

THE PACEMAKER

Dr Mark C Lidwell and Dr Edgar H Booth
Year: 1928
Location: Sydney

We've already mentioned the pacemaker in our medical section, and it's an interesting story. But it's worth noting here that Lidwell did not patent his 1928 design and has not always been credited as its original creator. For many years, American doctor Albert Hyman and his brother Charles were formally acknowledged as the inventors of the machine, which was released in 1932. This is probably due to the fact that the Americans invented the term 'artificial pacemaker' which caught the public's imagination and remains in use today.

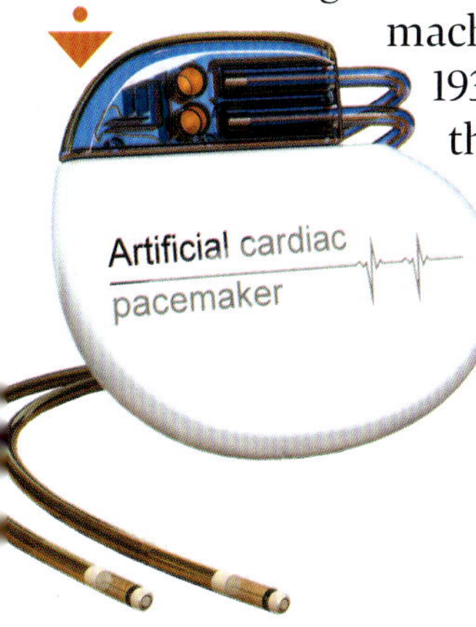

THE ARMOURED TANK

Lancelot de Mole
Year: 1911
Location: Adelaide

The prototype armoured tank, nicknamed Little Willie, was first engineered by the British in 1915 to address the trench warfare of World War I. The tank was designed to cross the combat zone and break into the defences of the enemy. Following further modifications, a second tank, nicknamed Big Willie, debuted at the First Battle of Somme in France. Adelaide-born Lancelot de Mole was key to the creation of the tank. In 1911, de Mole sent sketches and descriptions to the British War Office for his idea of an armoured vehicle that ran on continuous tracks. He received notice in 1913 that the British had rejected his idea. A British royal commission later acknowledged de Mole's design as a brilliant invention that surpassed Big Willie's design, but de Mole was never formally recognised as the tank's inventor.

WHAT'S THE BIG IDEA?

CHARITY EVENTS & SERVICES

CLEAN UP THE WORLD

Ian Kiernan
Year: 1993
Location: Sydney

Rather than just be upset by rubbish that littered beaches, harbours and oceans, Sydney yachtsman Ian Kiernan took action. In 1987, he gathered friends to spend the day cleaning Sydney Harbour. Clean Up Sydney Harbour Day, as he called it, was such a success that in 1990, Kiernan turned it into Clean Up Australia Day.

Kieran took his campaign to the world and launched Clean Up the World Day. Today more than 130 countries participate.

MOVEMBER

Travis Garone and Luke Slattery
Year: 2003
Location: Melbourne

In 2003, Travis Garone and Luke Slattery were chatting about moustaches when they decided to challenge friends to grow a mo. They charged each participant $10 and donated the money to a men's health charity. The event was so popular that Garone and Slattery turned it into an annual fundraising event each November and called it Movember.

MOVEMBER HAS RAISED MORE THAN $730 MILLION FOR MEN'S HEALTH PROGRAMS.

MOBILE LAUNDRY VAN FOR THE HOMELESS

Lucas Patchett and Nicolas Marchesi
Year: 2014
Location: Brisbane

More than 116,000 Australians don't have a place to call home. In 2014, school friends Lucas Patchett and Nic Marchesi offered people experiencing homelessness a free laundry service. As well as being somewhere for people to clean their clothes for free, the service also offered a safe place for people to connect.

What started with one van with two washing machines and two dryers quickly grew into an organisation called Orange Sky.

Orange Sky now also provides warm showers to those doing it tough, and helps people across Australia and New Zealand.

MORE THAN 116,000 AUSTRALIANS DON'T HAVE A PLACE TO CALL HOME.

EARTH HOUR, 2007

Andy Riley
Year: 2007
Location: Sydney

Climate change worried Australian man Andy Ridley so much that he decided to do something about it. He teamed up with the World Wildlife Fund to create Earth Hour, an event which raises awareness of climate change and encourages people to take action by switching off power for 60 minutes on one day of the year.

The first Earth Hour was in Sydney on March 31, 2007, and it has grown into a world-wide event, taking place at 8.30pm on the last Saturday in March.

Popular tourist attractions, including Sydney Harbour Bridge and New York's Times Square, take part in Earth Hour.

CHARITY EVENTS & SERVICES

TIMELINE

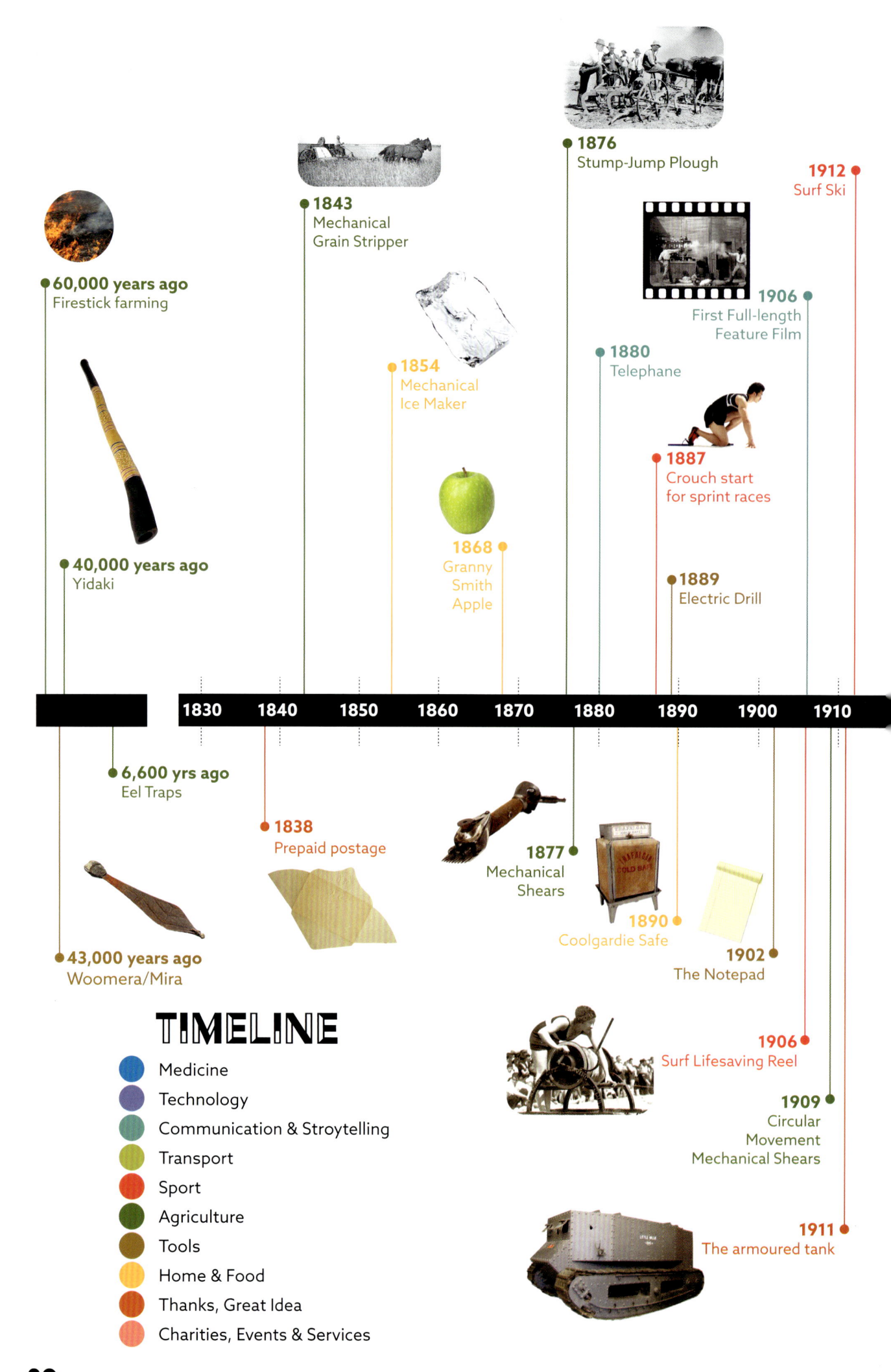

- **60,000 years ago** Firestick farming
- **40,000 years ago** Yidaki
- **43,000 years ago** Woomera/Mira
- **6,600 yrs ago** Eel Traps
- **1838** Prepaid postage
- **1843** Mechanical Grain Stripper
- **1854** Mechanical Ice Maker
- **1868** Granny Smith Apple
- **1876** Stump-Jump Plough
- **1877** Mechanical Shears
- **1880** Telephane
- **1887** Crouch start for sprint races
- **1889** Electric Drill
- **1890** Coolgardie Safe
- **1902** The Notepad
- **1906** First Full-length Feature Film
- **1906** Surf Lifesaving Reel
- **1909** Circular Movement Mechanical Shears
- **1911** The armoured tank
- **1912** Surf Ski

1830 1840 1850 1860 1870 1880 1890 1900 1910

TIMELINE

- Medicine
- Technology
- Communication & Stroytelling
- Transport
- Sport
- Agriculture
- Tools
- Home & Food
- Thanks, Great Idea
- Charities, Events & Services

32

TIMELINE

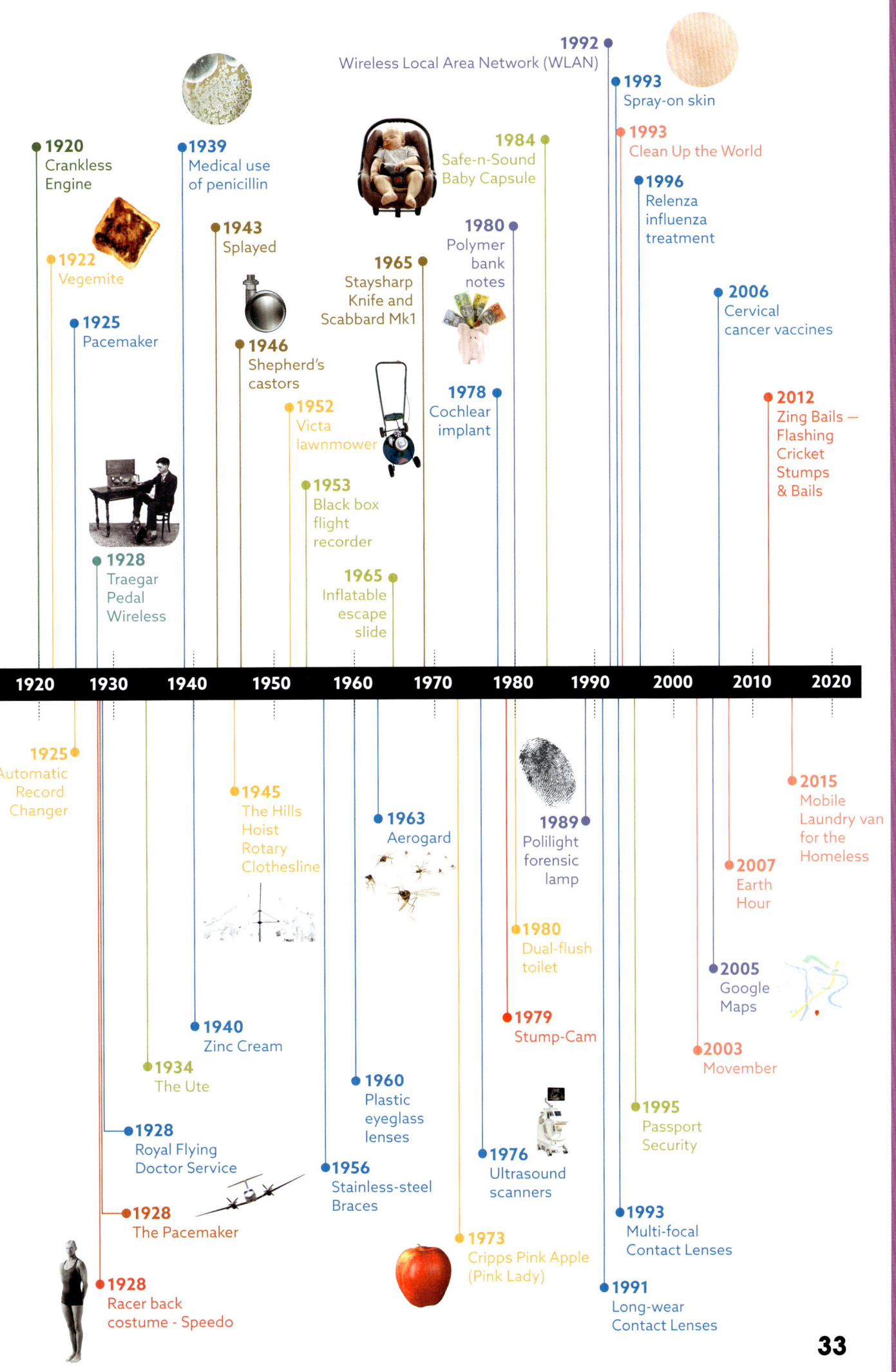

- **1920** Crankless Engine
- **1922** Vegemite
- **1925** Pacemaker
- **1925** Automatic Record Changer
- **1928** Traegar Pedal Wireless
- **1928** Royal Flying Doctor Service
- **1928** The Pacemaker
- **1928** Racer back costume – Speedo
- **1934** The Ute
- **1939** Medical use of penicillin
- **1940** Zinc Cream
- **1943** Splayed
- **1945** The Hills Hoist Rotary Clothesline
- **1946** Shepherd's castors
- **1952** Victa lawnmower
- **1953** Black box flight recorder
- **1956** Stainless-steel Braces
- **1960** Plastic eyeglass lenses
- **1963** Aerogard
- **1965** Staysharp Knife and Scabbard Mk1
- **1965** Inflatable escape slide
- **1973** Cripps Pink Apple (Pink Lady)
- **1976** Ultrasound scanners
- **1978** Cochlear implant
- **1979** Stump-Cam
- **1980** Polymer bank notes
- **1980** Dual-flush toilet
- **1984** Safe-n-Sound Baby Capsule
- **1989** Polilight forensic lamp
- **1991** Long-wear Contact Lenses
- **1992** Wireless Local Area Network (WLAN)
- **1993** Spray-on skin
- **1993** Clean Up the World
- **1993** Multi-focal Contact Lenses
- **1995** Passport Security
- **1996** Relenza influenza treatment
- **2003** Movember
- **2005** Google Maps
- **2006** Cervical cancer vaccines
- **2007** Earth Hour
- **2012** Zing Bails — Flashing Cricket Stumps & Bails
- **2015** Mobile Laundry van for the Homeless

33

GLOSSARY

Antibiotics – type of medicine that kill bacteria, but not viruses.

Aquaculture – the farming and breeding of water creatures such as fish, eels, shellfish and plants.

Climate change – name for changes to global temperatures.

Combustion engine – engine which burns fuel such as petrol to make it work.

Electrodes – a device that conducts electricity.

Horsepower – a way to measure power, usually in engines or motors. One unit of horsepower is what one horse can pull.

Influenza – contagious viral infection that affects the lungs.

Laminate – product made from many layers of a material.

Malaria – an infection passed to people by mosquitoes.

Patent – an official document that acknowledges the right of an inventor to have an exclusive right to make, use, and earn money from their invention.

Rootstock – a plant, often an underground part, onto which another variety of plant is grafted.

Scabbard – a cover for the blade of a dagger, sword or knife.

Sulphuric ether – this pale-yellow liquid is an organic solvent can easily catch fire.

WLAN – a wireless communication network that links devices to form a local area network.

INDEX

agriculture 18, 19, 20, 24, 28
Australian History 11, 17, 18, 19, 22
communication 11, 12, 17, 22, 29
charity/community 30, 31
environmental studies 30, 31
First Nations 11, 18, 19, 22
fashion 16, 19
film 11
first aid 3, 15
food technology 21, 23, 25, 26, 27
geography 10
history 29
music 26
outdoor education 5
science 3, 4, 5, 6, 7, 8, 13, 15, 16, 17, 29, 30
travel 14
transport 3, 10, 13, 14

writing 22